Otis

Loren Long

Otis

PHILOMEL BOOKS • PENGUIN YOUNG READERS GROUP

Patricia Lee Gauch, Editor

PHILOMEL BOOKS
A division of Penguin Young Readers Group.
Published by The Penguin Group.   Penguin Group (USA) Inc., 375 Hudson Street, New York, NY 10014, U.S.A.
Penguin Group (Canada), 90 Eglinton Avenue East, Suite 700, Toronto, Ontario M4P 2Y3, Canada (a division of Pearson Penguin Canada Inc.).
Penguin Books Ltd, 80 Strand, London WC2R 0RL, England.
Penguin Ireland, 25 St. Stephen's Green, Dublin 2, Ireland (a division of Penguin Books Ltd).
Penguin Group (Australia), 250 Camberwell Road, Camberwell, Victoria 3124, Australia (a division of Pearson Australia Group Pty Ltd).
Penguin Books India Pvt Ltd, 11 Community Centre, Panchsheel Park, New Delhi - 110 017, India.
Penguin Group (NZ), 67 Apollo Drive, Rosedale, North Shore 0632, New Zealand (a division of Pearson New Zealand Ltd).
Penguin Books (South Africa) (Pty) Ltd, 24 Sturdee Avenue, Rosebank, Johannesburg 2196, South Africa.
Penguin Books Ltd, Registered Offices: 80 Strand, London WC2R 0RL, England.

Published simultaneously in Canada.   Manufactured in China by South China Printing Co. Ltd.

Design by Semadar Megged.   Text set in 15.5-point Engine.
The art was created in gouache and pencil.

Library of Congress Cataloging-in-Publication Data
Long, Loren.   Otis / Loren Long.   p. cm.   Summary: When a big new yellow tractor replaces Otis, the friendly little tractor, he is cast away behind the barn, but it is only Otis who can come to the rescue when trouble happens.   [1. Tractors—Fiction. 2. Farm life—Fiction. 3. Farms—Fiction.] I. Title.   PZ7.L8555Ot 2009   [E]—dc22   2008050020
ISBN 978-0-399-25248-8
1 3 5 7 9 10 8 6 4 2

FOR TRACY, GRIFFITH AND GRAHAM.

There was once a friendly little tractor. His name was Otis, and every day Otis and his farmer worked together taking care of the farm they called home. Otis liked to work.

But after working hard all day, Otis was ready to unwind and play. He would ride the rolling hills and skirt Mud Pond down by the corn.

He would leapfrog bales of hay and explode through the haystacks.

On occasion, he would chase a rabbit or play ring-around-the-rosy
with the ducks to the sound of his steady *putt puff puttedy chuff.*
And sometimes, at the end of the day, he would just sit under
the apple tree and watch the farm below.

Every night, tired but happy, Otis would *putt puff* into the
little stall in the barn that was all his.

One night when Otis was fast asleep, the farmer brought a
beautiful baby calf into the barn. The calf bawled and bawled
for her mother, but when the sleepy sound of a soft *putt puff
puttedy chuff* came from the next stall, the scared little calf
stopped bawling and drifted off to sleep.

From that day on, the calf started following the little tractor wherever he went. *Putt puff puttedy chuff.* She followed him over the rolling hills and down by Mud Pond. She was right behind him leapfrogging bales of hay.

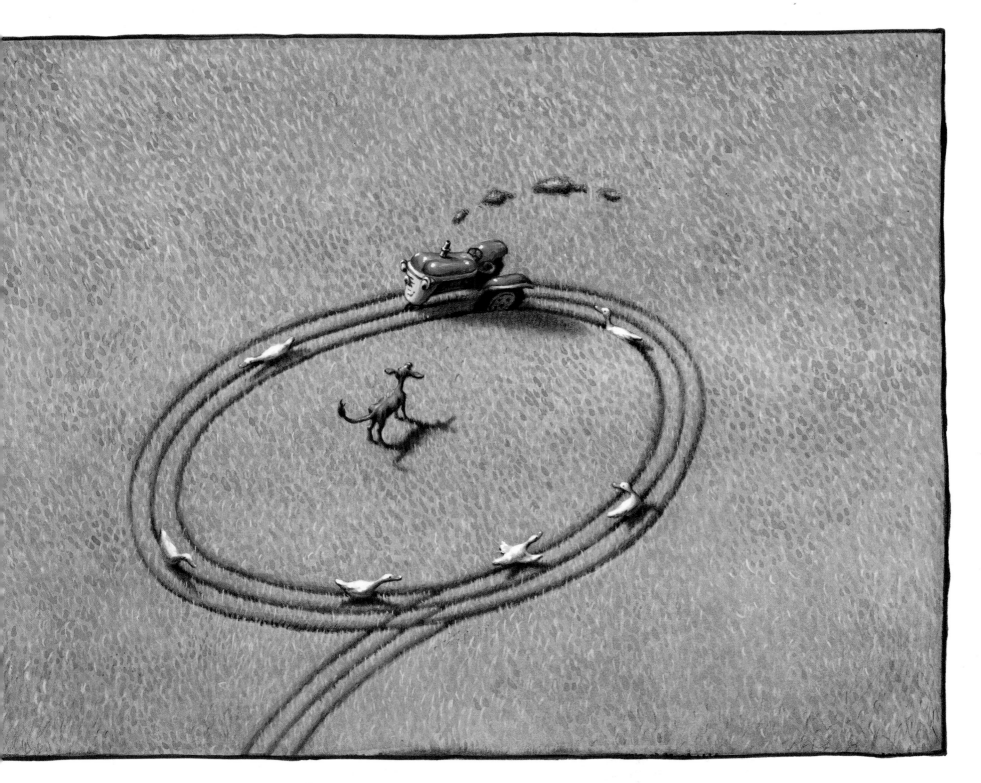

And the calf made their games of ring-around-the-rosy all the better.

Sometimes, at the end of the day, the two of them would just
sit together under the apple tree and watch the farm below.
Otis loved his little calf and the little calf loved Otis.

Then one day the farmer surprised everyone with a brand-new yellow tractor. "Time to move out, Otis," the farmer said.

He took Otis out of the little stall in the barn that was all his and parked him back behind the barn.

Then he backed the big yellow tractor into the stall next to the little calf.

But the little calf didn't like the big yellow tractor. He had a deep rumbling snore that shook the stall when he slept. There was no one to purr the little calf gently to sleep. No one to spend her days with.

And Otis? Otis could not even see his farm, as the weeds began to cover his tires. His friend often sat with him, but she could not get him to play like the old days.

It was early summer when the farmer discovered a poster: "Who has the prettiest calf in the land? Judges will decide at the County Fair and award a fancy blue ribbon to the winner!" The farmer knew the answer. He would show the little calf.

But on the morning of the fair, the little calf was nowhere to be found. She had wandered down to Mud Pond by the cornfield to cool off.

When she waded into the muddy water, her feet sank. With every step, she sank deeper and deeper and deeper.

The little calf was stuck in Mud Pond.

"Get the hands!" the farmer shouted when he saw her. All the farmhands came running with their ropes, but the more they tugged, the more stuck the calf got.

"Get the big yellow tractor!" the farmer shouted. "He can save
her." But the big tractor just scared the little calf. She sank in
deeper and deeper. Nearby farmers began to gather.

"Then call Fire Chief Douglas and the fire truck!" the farmer shouted. "They can save our little calf." But the sight of the big red fire truck startled the little calf in even deeper.

The farmer was fit to be tied . . . if the farmhands and the big tractor and even Fire Chief Douglas and his fire truck couldn't save the little calf, who could?

Suddenly, the little calf's ears perked up. Over the hum of the growing crowd, there came a faint sound in the distance . . . a soft rhythmic purr, *putt puff puttedy chuff.* The crowd turned and looked.

The sound became louder, putt puff puttedy chuff. And all at once, Otis *putt puff*ed from around the barn. He turned and headed straight toward Mud Pond.

Otis *putt puffed* down the rolling hill and pulled right up next to the muddy water's edge. The calf heard her friend's puttering purr and bawled. It was something like a hello.

Then to the sound of his gentle chuff and the amazement of all the people in the crowd, Otis slowly began to circle the pond.

He circled and he circled, and the little calf turned and turned,

never taking her eyes off of her friend.

With each ring Otis made around Mud Pond, the muddy grip loosened until the calf was able to stumble out of the pond on her own.

The two friends had found each other again.

Otis led the calf right down the dusty road toward the village. And everyone threw flowers as they went, following them into town. It looked like a happy parade.

No one needed a fancy blue ribbon to tell them that the calf was a special calf, Otis was a special tractor, and the two of them were special friends.

From that day on, the farmer discovered that with Otis's puttering purr beside the chicken coop, his chickens laid more eggs. At milking time, with Otis's gentle chuff nearby, his cows produced more milk. On occasion, Otis even got to join the farmer and the big yellow tractor out in the fields.

But often, at the end of the day, Otis would just sit with his friend under the apple tree and watch the farm below.

THE END